She's Not My Real Mother

Story and Pictures by
Judith Vigna

Albert Whitman & Company, Chicago

Other Books by Judith Vigna

Anyhow, I'm Glad I Tried

Couldn't We Have a Turtle Instead?

Everyone Goes as a Pumpkin

Gregory's Stitches

The Hiding House

The Little Boy Who Loved Dirt and
Almost Became a Superslob

Copyright © 1980 by Judith Vigna
Published simultaneously in Canada
by General Publishing, Limited, Toronto
All rights reserved. Printed in U.S.A.

Library of Congress Cataloging in Publication Data
Vigna, Judith.
    She's not my real mother.

    (A Concept book/level 1)
    SUMMARY: When Miles gets lost, his stepmother comes
to his rescue, forcing him to reevaluate her. Could she
be his friend?
    [1.   Stepmothers—Fiction]   I. Title.
PZ7.V67Sh   [E]   80-19073
ISBN 0-8075-7340-X

I spent last weekend at Daddy's place.

Mommy and Daddy don't live
together anymore. They got a divorce.

Daddy lives in the city with HER.

She's his new wife.

I don't like HER.
She's not my REAL mother.

But I like where Daddy
and she live.

Sometimes I go up and down,
up and down, all day
on the elevator.

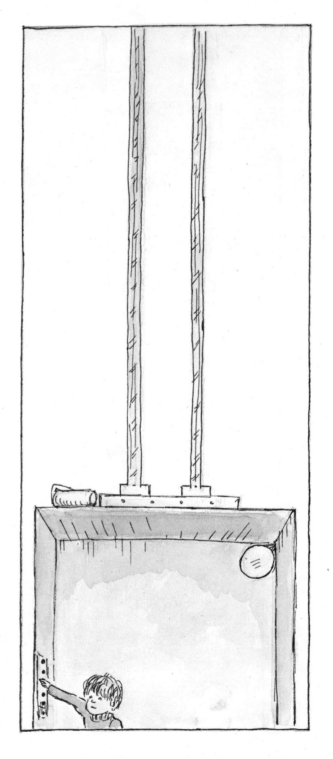

I like it when Daddy takes
me to the zoo.

Some of the animals are funny.

But I don't like it when SHE comes, too.
Saturday she bought me a balloon.
I wouldn't say thank you,
and Daddy got mad.

I didn't care.
She's not my real mother.

When we got back to Daddy's
apartment, SHE said, "I'd
like to be your friend."

I said, "Well, that's too bad.
I don't want to be yours!"

She looked sad,
but I wasn't sorry.

Not really.

Sunday morning, Daddy said,
"I've got some work to do today."

And SHE said, "Would you like
to go to the Ice Show with
me? There will be clowns and
skating bears. It'll be fun."

I didn't want to go to the Ice
Show with HER.

I wanted to go with Daddy.

But he said the Ice Show wouldn't
be here much longer, and if I
didn't go today, I'd have to
wait until next year.

So I thought I'd better go,
even without Daddy.

SHE and I took a bus to a big,
enormous place called a stadium.

There were clowns and skating bears.
She'd said there would be.

I liked the show a lot.

But I thought I'd better not
be too nice to her.
Suppose Mommy found out
and got mad and left me,
just the way Daddy did?
I'd practically be an orphan!

So when we went for popcorn,
I hid behind a column, just
to scare her a little.

She looked around and couldn't
see me.

She called my name a lot of times,
but I didn't come out.
Then she went away—to hunt for
me, I guess.

She was gone a long time.

She was gone so long I thought
I'd better go tell her I was
only pretending to be lost.

But I couldn't find her anywhere.

I thought maybe she'd gone
home without me.
I was all alone.
It was scary.

Then I heard a big voice over the loudspeaker, saying, "Will the little lost boy named Miles please go to the nearest guard?"

Everyone was looking for me. I was famous!

I saw a guard. "I'm the little lost boy," I told him.

He took me to a room
at the top of some steps.

She was there, waiting for me.
I was really glad to see her.

We went back to our seats for
the second half of the show.

I let her put her arm around me,
because she seemed nervous.

When we got back to Daddy's
apartment, he said, "Well, did
you two have a good time?"

She winked at me, and I knew
she wasn't going to tell Daddy
about the bad thing I did.

That was our secret.

So when it was time to go home,
I told her she could be
my friend.

I think that's what she wanted.

But Mommy doesn't have to worry—
she's my only REAL mother.